THE CREATOR

NP Novellas

Set 2:

Set 1:

THE CREATOR

Aliya Whiteley

NewCon Press
England

First published in the UK May 2025 by
NewCon Press
41 Wheatsheaf Road,
Alconbury Weston,
Cambs, PE28 4LF

NPN26 (limited edition hardback)
NPN27 (paperback)

10 9 8 7 6 5 4 3 2 1

ISBN:

978-1-912950-99-7 (hardback)
978-1-914953-98-9 (paperback)

Cover layout and design by Ian Whates
incorporating a photograph by MemoryCatcher

Editorial meddling and typesetting by Ian Whates

PART · ONE

Reynold was quite brilliant: the unparalleled inventor, creator, and scientific mind of our time. I could say unkind things about him, as a brother, and as one who attempted to be a confidante, if never quite daring to dream of becoming his equal. But that is a different story.

This is the story of Reynold's wife, and my dear friend, Patricia.

I remember the conversation we had, Reynold and I – this would have been in 1950? – at my club in Mayfair. He had pressed me for a meeting, which was unusual, and had driven in from Wantage. He even arrived early, greeting me at the member's bar with a firm handshake. How well he looked, how happy, as he broke the news of his engagement to one Patricia Alrington. We celebrated over dinner; the steak was tough, but there was good champagne, which I regretted later, as usual. But I was pleased to share in his happiness for a while, and his uncharacteristic loquaciousness was a joy. We hadn't had a good conversation since the war, and I missed it.

During dinner he said, "She is my saviour, you know. She has saved me."

"Not the religious type?" I joked.

"Not at all, not at all. Only that… there's an honesty to her that inspires me. I've spent my time trying to come up with ways to make myself a better man, and all this time she has been perfection, contained perfection, sitting quietly with her books and needlepoint. She needs nothing but to be in my company, and then she comes alive. Perhaps – do you think – less is more, when it comes to happiness? It lies in what we are, not what we achieve?" His cheeks were flushed, his eyes bright. "I'm saying this clumsily, Phillip, I…"

"You love her," I said.

"When you meet her, you'll love her too."

I replied, "She sounds wonderful. I'm so glad, so glad you've finally discovered a life outside of the laboratory."

I was in my late thirties, and he was approaching forty; I certainly thought my own chances of finding somebody to spend my years with were shrinking. He must have divined the direction of my thoughts and sympathised, in a rare moment, for he said, "Yes, we can both still change, perhaps."

But a month after the wedding, which was a quiet affair at her family's estate in Sussex, Patricia sent me a charming invitation to attend lunch at Wantage, and when I arrived I found Reynold ensconced in his laboratory, below stairs, as if nothing had changed at all.

"I'm so sorry, Phillip," she said. "Time must have slipped away from him. And he did promise me... but you know how important his work is."

I realised this meeting had been her idea, not his. We had managed only the barest of introductions at the wedding. I gathered, judging by her side of the church, that she had few relatives: a mother and father, getting on in years. No siblings.

"I do indeed," I said. "Without it, he wouldn't be Reynold."

She smiled, and I could see puzzlement in her eyes. Perhaps I had let some emotion slip through my words. I commented on the rose garden, heavy in bloom, beneath the north terrace, where we were sitting. The scent of the open flowers rose up, warm in the sunshine. It was a very beautiful day.

But beauty: this is a quality I've come to appreciate less and less. What does it matter that they were a handsome couple, considering the events that followed? What did it possibly matter, that their son, born before the end of that decade, was the perfect mixture of them both? I was appointed the role of godfather – there were no other godparents – and I felt an inexplicable pride in little Bucky. I doted on every milestone, from the first time he smiled at me. I suppose we had shared genes to account for my emotional response: those deep-set eyes, and the peak of the hair that looked distinguished on Reynold and rather clownish on myself. The truth is, I think, that it was Patricia's influence upon our family line that I was drawn to. The soft bow of the mouth, and the delicate lobes of the ear, and also something of her expression – that gentle slope of the eyebrows that felt calm, forgiving. Even as a newborn, Bucky shared those qualities.

I remember when I became his godfather – a role I have taken seriously although I am not much of a believer myself, after all I have seen – and I held him in my arms, standing before the font in the little Norman church in the village, only a few miles from the house in which we had grown up. It was one of those changeable days, heavy with clouds that scudded across the sky at speed, and the interior of St Mary's was dim, dusty, the cobwebs in evidence high in the rafters. Behind the font was the pride of the parish, sustained with our family's money: five panels of stained glass, showing the annunciation, the visitation, the nativity, the adoration of the magi, and the presentation: that fascinating story of old. I had not paid much attention to those panels for an age, but as the water was tipped over Bucky's head it seemed to me he looked up and wondered at them, and the clouds sped past the sun so that light flooded the church, illuminating us all in the reds, greens, blues of the expertly shaped glass.

Bucky stared and stared. His captivation was evident.

All a fiction on my part, this assignation of personality on to the blank sheet of a baby? Yes, probably. But I wondered, later, if Reynold had harboured similar thoughts about the influences innate that would turn the boy into a man. Perhaps that philosophical question of nature versus nurture had played some part in the terrible events that followed.

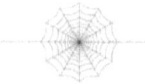

Reynold, it was safe to say, took after our father. No doubt you have heard of Thomas Corbus: adventurer, writer, diarist and raconteur, and the creator of the Air Pocket – that marvellous invention in the form of a trapped bubble of warmed air within two giant transparent spheres, one inside the other, cradled in a very odd-looking, giant device: a pouch strung between tall posts that reach far into the sky. The elastic properties of the cables attached to the pouch, combined with the rotation of the outer sphere, are sufficient to fling the passenger nearly to the edge of the atmosphere. Our father described it as a vertiginous view that becomes meaningless as one gets higher and the blue of the sky fades to black. Reynold said much the same, on his own trip, undertaken on his fifteenth birthday. The sphere would then crack open at the touch of an installed button, and parachutes would ensure a safe landing, but nothing would persuade me to try it myself. Fear, and the inability to tame it: that was my mother's gift to me. She stayed at home, suffered from headaches if anything occurred out of her routine. As young men my brother and I pitied her, or shared our mutual irritation when yet another attack came along.

My own headaches did not start until after the war. I served in Europe and gave my undistinguished best; Reynold was mainly in the east. We returned bright and bold, seemingly untouched by the horrors, but the pains started for me within weeks. Now I understand that our mother was worthy of the respect we gave our father so easily, and more. Pain is beyond a debilitation or a weakness of character. It is the ever-present threat that your thoughts will not be your own, and your body cannot be relied upon. I make constant deals with myself that I cannot keep. I say *I will no longer drink wine*, or *I will remember not to squint into the sunlight*, and so the list grows of things that may or may not cause an attack, and the list is always of things that I love and do not want to give up. I persevere, and persevere, making myself miserable, until the moment someone smiles at me, and says, *sit in the garden, drink this champagne*, and the high, the high of it! Then it exacts its price, and I lie in the dark for a day.

Or the pain comes for no reason, the deal was never worth making in the first place. And that is worse, I think. Yes, that is worse.

Anyway, the lunch at Wantage: there was wine, there was sunshine. I partook of both. The north terrace has a wonderful view down to the lake, and the woods beyond. She had a salad served, light but tasty, with chicken and grapes.

"I don't have much to do with the garden, I admit," Patricia said. "The gardeners come three times a week, as they have for years. I don't interfere."

"Knowing when to become involved and when to leave well alone is a ridiculously underappreciated trait," I said. "Look at the results. A wonderful garden, a house running smoothly. And Reynold is so happy."

My comment made her smile, and I was glad, for we both knew and would not speak of how she had not managed to change him after all, and he was unassailable in that laboratory of his. So soon after the marriage, too.

"Hasn't he always been happy?" she asked me, lightly. "He has his work. I make a comment about the weather, or show him something in a book I'm reading, and he gets that look, rushes to make a note, or disappears for days. I don't think I could take any credit for the latest great invention to come, and I would never expect to."

"If your conversation inspired him, then I think you should be permitted to call yourself a muse, at the very least," I told her. I can picture her as if it took place yesterday. She wore a simple dress, with a scarf bearing a print of green leaves and yellow tulips tied loosely around her neck. We sat at the head of the long white table, laid with a clean tablecloth and cutlery for many more people, the silverware gleaming; this was to have been a large occasion, and I realised she must have cancelled everyone else's attendance when she got wind of Reynold's refusal to appear. I was flattered. Perhaps she had pleaded with him, through that thick door at the bottom of the stairs that formed a barrier with the outside world, kept his laboratory utterly private, with no result. I felt sorry for her, then, and was reminded of my mother, who stayed and was ignored for years in this very house. How could Patricia bear the same fate? Possibly we all look at each other's choices and wonder how they can be lived with. Her thoughts lay on similar lines to my own, I guessed, for she said, then, quietly, "Reynold told me of your headaches."

"They come and go." Then, in the spirit of honesty, I added, "One is coming now, I'm afraid."

"Oh, I'm sorry, I'm so sorry, I – was it the food? Can I help, at all?"

I felt shabby for mentioning it. One of the parts of illness that I know well is the shame of inconveniencing others. I apologised, and she waved it away.

"You know," she said, "I have an excellent doctor, and I mentioned your condition – he said he knew someone who might be able to help. I can give you his telephone number –"

"You spoke on my behalf?" I didn't know whether to feel pleased she had considered me, or aghast to be discussed as an invalid.

"I saw him yesterday in London, and you came up in conversation – I had to shop for lunch, and I said you'd be attending. I do hope you don't mind."

I'd flustered her, and apologised in turn, then wished for a world without apologies. How excruciating it could be: politeness. But she had seen a doctor, and I said, alarmed, "But you're not ill yourself?"

She put a hand to her stomach, and said with a small smile that no, and I should not worry, and that was how I found out about the existence of my nephew Buckingham, so early in his life and their marriage.

I changed the subject, and we went on through lunch. I should have left while still capable of driving, but in truth I think I wanted to stay, regardless of consequences. The headache swelled. It was the type that narrows my vision to a point – without much immediate pain at first. I watched her as if through a long tunnel until the throbbing started in my temple, and I could no longer manage conversation. Driving was indeed out of the question.

"Stay here, until it passes," she said. "I'll have the curtains drawn in the guest room. Stay as long as you want. What can I fetch for you? Water? Ice wrapped in a cloth?"

I tried to get up and blundered, hit the edge of the table, knocking over my empty glass. She took my arm and led me into the house, up the stairs, to the room that had once been my grandmother's chamber. It had been furnished with heavy oak wardrobe and chest of drawers, gold framed portraits, and thick draped clothes over the poster bed, but was now repurposed as a bland guest room with two single beds and plain walls. Only the old washstand remained, in the corner by the window, as a nod to the past, perhaps.

She drew the curtains and left me, and with the last of my vision I took off my jacket and tie and fell to one of the beds. I thought of nothing else but the pain, then, until later at night – very late – when I came around with the sudden wakefulness that often characterises the period after the headache, bringing clarity. I thought back over Patricia's condition, her small smile, and suddenly felt quite sure that she had not yet told Reynold, and I was the very first to know. I can't say why I thought that, or that I was pleased or displeased. I only knew it.

I rose, got dressed, took the stairs quietly. The house was very quiet, in the grip of sleep. I hesitated, then took the final flight downwards to Reynold's sanctum. As I suspected, the laboratory door was closed. I could not have entered anyway, for health reasons. But I knocked, and wondered if Reynold might emerge, and come to the smaller lounge with me for a brandy.

There was, as ever, no answer.

What would I have said, if he had answered the door that night? Would I have asked what new inspiration had come to him, and why it took priority over the needs of his new bride? As the less important brother, could I have dared to tell him how very lucky he was?

We've had money, connections, everything, for many generations. Who else but a rich man gets to declare themselves an inventor? At least Father had the grace to be good at it. When his flying ball was a success, he formed a charity offering scholarships to disadvantaged boys, providing the funds to attend our old school. He managed this himself, and I took over after his death. *Find the brilliant,* he said in the written instructions he left.

I've always known what brilliance looks like. I saw it every day, in my father, then in my brother. But Reynold concentrated on attempting to understand how brilliance erupts; that is, how one comes across inspiration, how a brain envisages that which has never existed before, and that led him to the invention that cemented his reputation as a genius in his early twenties, before Patricia, before the war, even: the ThinkBulb. I never cared for the name myself, but could not deny that it was an astounding piece of technology – a thick nest of metal strands, powered by electric current, that could be embedded into the walls, floors and ceilings of any building in order to stimulate creative thinking. How it works, I have no notion, but businesses all over the world continue to swear by it. Boardrooms, offices and lecture halls had it fitted, and reported their employees and students were brighter, quicker, more engaged. Sometimes I saw advertisements for it in the newspapers, saying:

INSPIRE YOURSELF

It was not recommended for people with certain health conditions, and I was advised to steer clear. Reynold had it installed in his own laboratory – and who could blame him? But it did mean the place was off-limits to me, and our lives were even less connected as a result. Looking back at it all now, I wonder if he had always wanted it that way. If he had known I could not have approved of the direction in which his ceaseless mind led him, and how it would jeopardise his family.

I did not get out to Wantage again for some time, being given no invitation to attend. I made the occasional telephone call, and the housekeeper took messages. Patricia telephoned me back once or twice, and sent a letter with best wishes in the few lines. I worried about them both, but I devoted myself to the charity, and also to my painting. My career progressed modestly: an exhibition here, a few sales there. I cherished these small victories, and wondered if Reynold would have understood the joy of scaling the hillocks when the mountains came so easily to him.

Art was not a childhood passion of mine. It was only when my attempts at a more traditional career – upon demobilisation – were stymied by my condition that I chose to adopt a path that offered a more forgiving schedule and an outlet for my emotions. Not that my paintings are bleak or self-reflective; I love nature in all its forms, and I paint it as I find it. I have never had an attack during the days spent with my travelling easel and paints, deep in the woods or on the banks of a river. I strive to capture the world faithfully. I work in oils, and texture is everything. How deep, how dense and saturated the landscape is, in light, in colour! I layer, I slather, I can become frenzied towards the end of the process. Something of it feels separate from me, as if it comes from the divine.

See? I, too, suffer the egotism of the creator. Perhaps I have more in common with Reynold than I ever thought.

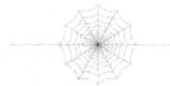

Buckingham was born in the spring of 1951, and I was informed by telephone only a few days afterwards. Reynold was effusive, overjoyed. He invited me to the house. I drove up that weekend, and it was as if no time had passed, yet everything had changed. Reynold watched Bucky, tended to Patricia's needs. It was a cold April, I remember, and all the fires in the house were lit. He brought her broth, and there was tea for me; he poured it himself. We sat together in the lounge, talked of how clever and handsome Bucky would be, all the signs of greatness already upon him, in his wide eyes and tightly closed fists, and Reynold did not mention his work once.

Patricia looked pale, utterly tired, but content. I knew a little something about what is left on the other side of pain and fear – the clarity such experiences bring. I wondered what she had learned about herself.

Regardless of that, I think I left them truly happy. That thought sustains me, now, knowing what dark times were to come. They did know happiness.

Bucky grew into a fine chap, and I saw as much of him as I could. My attacks eased off in frequency at that time, and in the summer before my fine nephew left for boarding school – a prospect that excited him greatly but left me feeling a little bereft at how quickly the years were passing us by – I spent as much time at the house as I could, at Patricia's encouragement. She commented on how much good Bucky's presence seemed to do me.

She was absolutely right: he was a tonic. We played tennis and croquet, and when we tired of those games we took to the woods. Hide-and-seek, and tag, and poking through the undergrowth for small animals, or insects. I bought him a notebook and strung a small glass jar on twine so he could keep his finds around his neck and draw them, then release them back into the wild. Snails, spiders, centipedes: he gave them all serious attention, and had the makings of a talented sketcher, I thought. I remember one sketch of a gorgeous specimen: an orb web spider. Many of them lived in the woods, stringing webs from branch to branch, and this one was a mighty size, large in the jar. It was very still once captured, I recall, giving the impression of being aware of its predicament. It would save its energy to then throw itself bodily against the glass, loud enough to be heard, before retreating to stillness once more, as if considering another plan of escape. But that quality made it a perfect artistic subject. Bucky captured something of its colouring and markings with diligence: that pattern upon its back, symmetrical, suggestive of a rage-filled face designed to scare predators away. It created a feeling that the spider observed one, rather than one observing the spider. Curious, and disconcerting.

Yes, as much as he had energy to spare, and loved to run free for hours, he could also be a solemn young man, much given to inspection of the things that surrounded him. He had no fear, and I saw both the artist and scientist nascent within him.

Then we would return to the terrace and find his mother, and show her his latest finds and drawings. She praised him, and asked him questions, and then gave the order for early dinner to be served, and it was as if Reynold did not exist at all. I often wished him to emerge from his laboratory and realise what he was missing.

Patricia often walked me to my car after those dinners, and I took to parking further down, by the wrought iron gates, so we could both get a little exercise and chat about events of the day. We were not confidantes. Our talk was light, never of personal issues. Perhaps the closest we came was the time that I dared to ask, as we strolled side by side with the gravel crunching underfoot, "Does Bucky visit his father in the laboratory?"

"No, not especially," she said. "You know how Reynold hates to be disturbed, and he tells me he's close to a breakthrough now. But he emerges most nights to tell Bucky a story at bedtimes, and wish him sweet dreams."

"But Bucky has been down there?"

She did not reply, at first. Then she said, "You worry about the ThinkBulb."

"Bucky is so bright, so attentive. Do you think it…?"

"He's a healthy little boy," she said, with a sharpness to her tone that surprised me.

"Of course," I said. "Forgive me."

"There's nothing to forgive. We all have his best interests at heart. You are a wonderful uncle and godfather, and it has cheered me to see you two become such firm friends. And you, looking so well!"

"Thank you." I felt compelled to add, "I've had periods such as this before. It won't last, I'm afraid, but I will enjoy it while I can."

"Then so will I."

We were almost at the car. The tall avenue of silver lime trees threw long shadows as the sun fell lower, and a cold breeze blew. The long road beyond stretched back to London, and my small room at the club. I had the urge to say: *I will stay the night, come, let's get Reynold and Bucky, let's all of us go into the woods and hunt for small things in the fading light.*

Patricia said, suddenly, "Does it bother you?"

"What's that, my dear?"

"That he never once tried to cure your headaches?"

How could I answer? It hit the centre of my most selfish, secret thoughts. I reached for her hand, and she gave it. I squeezed her soft palm with my own.

She said, "Perhaps we are lucky he's never turned his attention to the problem of fixing us. We would not be the same, would we? He changes all he touches."

"Patricia," I told her. "There's nothing about you that needs fixing."

"Nor you," she replied.

We held hands for a moment longer, a gesture of mutual support, of understanding: my acquired sister, and I. Then we broke apart. I climbed into the car, and rolled down the window. She crouched a little, and said, "Thank you for coming."

"It's my pleasure."

"It's the nature of gods among men to be capricious," she said, then, suddenly. "They must do as their hearts tell them."

I did not care for that sentiment. "Reynold is not a god," I said. "I shared a room with him when we were boys, and he used to blow his nose and put his dirty handkerchief under my pillow. That's not godlike behaviour. Although one could say it's capricious."

She laughed, and stood back. I drove to London with my attention barely on the road.

Not long after that Bucky left for school – the alma mater – and there was no obvious reason to visit Wantage, for a while.

I never did ask her what she thought needed fixing about herself.

Would I have liked Reynold to turn to the problem of fixing my headaches? Of changing me in the process? Yes, absolutely, a hundred times yes.

It was a summer evening in 1958 when she telephoned me at my club.

"Reynold has killed himself," she said.

She sounded – not calm. But not distraught.

I said, "Has there been an accident?" and she replied, "Bucky is home. Can you come?" The call ended. I could picture her, standing in the hall, her back to the dining room, putting the receiver into place. I imagined her eyes on the portrait that could be seen from that vantage point, in the main lounge, hanging over the fire. It was of the three of them, painted when Bucky was a fine young man who had just learned to walk, with a jolly sailor suit and cap to match.

It made no sense.

Had she taken to drinking? No, no, she was never the type, and I would have heard it in her voice. I told myself there was a mistake, and I would be able to fix it. I ordered the car brought round. No doubt Reynold had locked himself in the laboratory for days on end, this time, and did not answer when she knocked. I would arrive, reason with him, and he would emerge full of annoyance, but also excitement for the grand new discovery he had made. There would be smiles, relief.

I could not fathom why Bucky was home. Surely the term did not finish until July. He had attended for three years now, and when I came to see him, I found myself admiring a tall and boisterous lad whom I didn't really know at all. He was keen on sport; he played in many matches. There was no reason for him to be home. He would not have come willingly, surely.

I made the journey in under an hour, feeling the beginnings of a headache crawling up my right cheek, into my brain.

When I reached the turning to the drive, I saw a sight that gave me a shock, brought on by circumstance, no doubt: a spirit! A spirit, hovering by the gates! But no, no, it became Patricia's face peering at me, waiting for me; how different she looked. She was dressed in a blouse and long skirt, bleached white by the headlights, with that small tulip-print scarf tied around her neck. She resembled both a ghost and a bride, her huge eyes shining. I worried for her sanity, but when I stopped the car and threw open the passenger door she climbed in, and I could see she was very much in control of herself. She said, "I'm sorry if I gave you a turn, but I couldn't be in the house alone. I'm sure you understand."

"But I thought Bucky was with you?"

"He's in the woods," she said, as if that was the only sensible place to be, so late on a summer night.

"Should we go and look for him?"

"He's happy there," she said. "I think it's for the best, for the moment. Reynold needs you more."

"Then Reynold is not…" I couldn't bring myself to say it.

Patricia put her cool little hand over mine, on the gearstick. "He's quite dead, Phillip."

"I don't understand," I said. The pain in my head was growing. We reached the house, all lit up, and I parked directly outside the front door. She was quick to leave the car, and she headed straight for the stairs to the laboratory.

"He's down there, then," I said. Where else would he be?

She hesitated. "Part of him remains there," she said.

The house was very quiet; where had all the staff gone? How empty it seemed. I could never remember a time it had been so devoid of life; as a boy, there had always been someone close by, fulfilling a duty or keeping an eye on me.

"I – Patricia –" I pressed my hand to my head, trying to think. "Forgive me, but I cannot go down there if the ThinkBulb is on. It's bad for my condition, and I'm already –"

"You're ill," she said, "Of course, the stress, oh, I should have thought of that, but you must, you must..."

"Can you turn it off? Where is the power?"

"I don't know. Wait. Wait here." She brushed past me and returned to the hall. I heard her footsteps moving away from me, growing distant. Then the lights of the hall and the stairwell snapped off, and a profound darkness enveloped me. Usually I find the absence of light soothing, but this change was too sudden, too unexpected: the pain in my head redoubled, sparked through me, and I had to steel myself against nausea. Footsteps, returning, bringing a small circle of light, and Patricia was beside me: "Come," she said, "I've switched off the main circuit, come." She took my hand, pointed her battery torch to the stairs, and we went down to the familiar blank wall of the laboratory door.

It was open.

His sanctum, open.

At that moment I understood that something terrible really had happened to Reynold.

Patricia kept her hand in mine. She swung the beam of the torch around as if searching for something: what? I could not help it; I called out his name; darkness swallowed the sound.

"Reynold!"

There was no response. The beam fell over the long table in the centre of the room, thick with scientific instruments in a row and papers, in a stack. I had not imagined he worked so neatly. Three filing cabinets crouched against one wall. The light caught a flash of a white form: no, no, it was a lab coat, hanging from a hook beside the cabinets, and beside that stood a tall stool with metallic, tubular legs. Then the beam split, bounced strangely; it had hit two glass screens erected around the stool, from the floor to the black beams across the ceiling, creating a booth into which one might enter, sit upon the stool. Dangling from the beams was a silver device, conical in shape, widening at the bottom. A helmet, of sorts. Wires protruded from the point where it was suspended, and more wires snaked down the sides and over the floor. The beam followed the wires to another set of glass screens surrounding a second stool. A duplicate? But the wires connected them.

"What is he working on?" I said, quietly.

"I can't begin to explain it now," she said, taking her hand from mine. The beam of the torch steadied on the far corner, along from the second stool. There was a green screen, rather like the ones found in hospitals and surgeries, and it was folded back to reveal a plinth, tall and solid, as high as my chest. Upon it sat a sculpture, or, rather, a block of clay left incomplete in the process of becoming a sculpture. It would, eventually, be a bust – that much was obvious from the shape – but the head and neck looked blank from this position, and the clay had that curiously dull quality that it possesses before the real work of shaping begins.

Patricia moved to the sculpture, taking the light with her. I followed to gain a better view of the head: eyes, nose and mouth. Here the act of transformation was closer to completion. A third of a face could be seen. The features were proud, handsome. One finished eye contained a hard glint of playful intelligence, and the line of the brow made something in my throat catch. It was Reynold's likeness.

"He… made this?"

"In a way."

The other eye was only lightly pressed into the clay, and on the cheeks were blotches, raised lumps, in a pattern; there was design to it. The more I looked upon it in the torchlight, the more I could discern delicate touches with a knife that surprised me. Small knobs, perfectly round, were spaced evenly across the forehead and also the back of the head, as if made with the precision of a machine. Each had a slightly thicker line to the upper curve, and a faint circle within. It came to me that they were also eyes: eyes, around the whole head, and they too contained something of Reynold's personality; it was as if he watched me in many ways, from numerous angles, and for a moment I saw myself through them, standing close to Patricia, and I felt – I felt his lofty intelligence observing me as a lesser being in his territory, and wondering what to do about me. It was a fearsome emotion, and I felt certain the clay had been sculpted precisely to convey that feeling. It was, with only half a human face upon monstrous mutation, complete in its own way. Reynold was a better artist than I had ever been.

"This is what's left of him," Patricia whispered. Her hands were pulling at the scarf around her throat, twisting in the material. There was horror and pain in her voice, deep and untouchable. But I could not let her emotions stop me from getting to the truth.

"Where is he?" I said, then, so there could be no room for misunderstanding, "Where is his body?" I took the torch from her fingers and swung it around the laboratory, into every nook, every shadow. He was not there. The pain in my head was excruciating.

"Oh Phillip," she said. "I promise you, this is all that remains, now."

There was nothing to do but take the stairs back up to the hall. She left me there as she switched on the electricity, and the blazing lights made me cry out. I managed to call the police, asked for assistance, an ambulance, anything. The operator assured me help was on the way. Then I stumbled to the closest bathroom and was sick, and put my head to the cool marble floor, and was lost to the world for a while.

A knock on the door brought me back to myself.

"Phillip?" It was Patricia, her voice hesitant, strained. "Are you… could you possibly…?"

"Yes," I said. "Yes." I got up, tucked in my shirt, adjusted my tie. The headache had vanished, as they do sometimes, leaving only a fading memory of pain ungraspable, like a time in the far past that could not be precisely recalled.

"The police need to speak to you. They say it's quite urgent, I'm afraid."

It all came back to me. The sculpture. The eyes. Reynold.

I looked at my own reflection in the bathroom mirror. How strange it was, that I was just the same; there was no sign of my thoughts, my worry for my brother. My face looked like that of a stranger. And there was no time to waste. I opened the door, and found her hovering there, her arms tightly folded over her chest. I said, "I'm so sorry to have left you alone, that was the last thing I wanted. Have they only just arrived?"

"They've been here a little while," she said. "There was an ambulance as well, but that's gone. There are two gentlemen in the morning room. Are you – in a lot of pain?"

"Don't worry about me," I said, as gently as I could.

She closed her eyes, swayed on her feet. I put out a hand, caught her arm, squeezed it. "They want to speak to you alone," she said. "I'll go and make some tea."

I let her go, and she walked away from me with carefully placed steps. She reminded me of a ballet dancer, or perhaps a tightrope walker with a long way to fall.

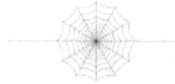

The morning room was my favourite in the house. My mother wrote most of her correspondence there; she had a number of friends whom she never saw in person, but they all exchanged letters regularly throughout their lives. She often had small cakes on a plate by her desk. She would pretend not to notice when I sneaked one and crammed it into my mouth. I was forever welcome: her youngest.

I squared my shoulders and strode in – the desk still in place before the bookshelf, the old chaise longue, a pair of upholstered armchairs in front of the unlit fire – and greeted the two policemen who awaited me. They stood before the velvet green curtains drawn over the bay window. One was young, tall, in uniform, his helmet tucked under his arm so his elbow protruded at an awkward angle. He looked new to the uniform, I thought. The other was my own height, with a bushy moustache of grey tinged with a fiery red, and shiny cheeks above a wide smile. He wore a

38

tweed houndstooth suit, and when he held out his hand to me with a brisk motion I could see the jacket was too short in the arm. His cufflink was in the shape of a small boat, the sail unfurled; I wondered if he was once a navy man. "Phillip Corbus?" he asked me.

I shook his hand. "Yes, that's right."

"Inspector Price, sir. This is Constable Davis. You telephoned the emergency number earlier?"

"Yes – I – what time is it now?" I checked my wristwatch as, simultaneously, Davis said, "It's just past midnight now, sir."

"We spoke to Mrs Corbus, and she tells us that her husband, Mr Reynold Corbus, that is, has taken his own life. I'm sorry to be blunt about it, but I think it's better if we speak plainly."

"She said the same thing to me."

"It's a very sad business. I'm afraid it's complicated by the fact that we haven't been able to find a – to find Mr Corbus – to ascertain precisely what's occurred, sir."

"I… yes, I can see that would be necessary, of course."

"Have you seen him yourself, at all?"

"No. No, Patricia was waiting for me at the gate when I arrived, and she took me straight into the house, and down to the laboratory. I thought he would be there, you know, he was usually there."

"Yes, we've checked the house. Mrs Corbus was happy for us to do that."

"But she still hasn't been able to say where he is?"

Inspector Price stroked his moustache. "Could you talk us through precisely what she's said to you about this business, sir?"

"Well… let's see…" I wished the fire had been lit; it would have been a comfort. I moved to the grate, put one hand on the mantelpiece. "She telephoned my club and broke the news. She seemed quite calm, I thought."

Davis took out a notepad and the stub of a blunt pencil from his top pocket. He flipped the pad open and began to make notes.

"Shock can do that, can't it? Keep one calm. Life or death situations," I said.

"Indeed it can," agreed Price. We exchanged a look of mutual understanding. Yes, he'd seen active service; I felt certain of it.

I thought back over the conversation. "She said Reynold had killed himself."

"Killed himself: that was the phrase she used?"

"Exactly so. There was no room for doubt."

"She didn't say he had left, for instance? Or she feared he was dead?"

"No. I'm certain of it."

"And did you see your brother when you arrived?"

"No, I thought Patricia was taking me to… well, he was inseparable from his laboratory." I was repeating myself, but Price only nodded. Then he asked, "Is Mrs Corbus quite well?"

I knew she had always struggled with her health, but the meaning under the words was clear to me. I had no qualms in telling him, "She has always been clear-minded and in control of her actions, Inspector." How strange it was, to stand there discussing her, while my brother was somewhere close, somewhere unknown to us. Alive or dead. Poised between the two. "Have you searched the house thoroughly?" I asked.

"We did, sir. The ambulance workers stayed as long as they could. They were concerned for Mrs Corbus, really, I think. That's standard protocol, with reports of this nature, and she agreed to be examined, given the situation. They said there's nothing physically untoward. Sometimes, in domestic situations, there are issues. Injuries." The young constable looked down, adjusted his collar, and Price continued, "Nothing of that nature here. And she told them their services weren't needed. You're well yourself, sir?"

I waved the question away. "Just a headache. An old ailment from the war."

"Did your brother suffer any similar problems?"

"Not at all. He was always fighting fit. Fighting fit."

"So you've had no concerns about either of them."

"None. Not until Patricia telephoned, and said about Reynold, and that Bucky was home –"

"Bucky?" said Price.

"Buckingham. Their son. He's only eight or so. He should be at school, but Patricia said he was here."

"Tea's ready," said Patricia, loudly, from the doorway. "Please, let's all sit down, I've found some biscuits. It's the housekeeper's night off but

I poked in some cupboards and found a stash. It's been quite the adventure." She carried the laden tray over to the occasional table by the bookcase. Cups, saucers, teaspoons, a bowl of sugar lumps, and a large workmanlike teapot that I'd no doubt belonged to the staff. She had arranged the biscuits in a fan configuration on a side plate.

"That's very kind of you, Mrs Corbus," said Price. He watched her fuss with the cups for a moment, then said, his voice quite gentle, "I wonder if we could speak to your son?"

"But he's asleep." She turned from the tray, towards me, speaking directly to me as if I held any power at that moment. "I can't wake him now, surely you understand that? Let him sleep until the morning, please. He'll wake to such terrible news."

It was a surprise; Bucky had returned to the house, then, while I was in the bathroom. I had questions, but I couldn't bear this eruption of desperation. "Of course," I said, although it was not my decision to make. "Surely that's acceptable, Inspector?" I appealed to him, and he was a good man. He hesitated but nodded.

"We can return in the morning and see if we can shed some light on the matter. Thank you for your kind offer of the tea, Mrs Corbus, but perhaps we should let you turn in for the night. You'll stay here overnight, sir? I'd advise that."

His words were curiously weighed. I realised it was not a request as much as a thinly veiled instruction, and I could understand it. Patricia obviously could not be left alone.

"Absolutely," I assured him.

The constable was looking longingly at the tray. Patricia's eyes were on him. She poured a cup, put two lumps of sugar in it with a generous splash of milk, and passed it to Davis with three biscuits. "Here,' she said, "Drink it down quickly, and I'm sure the inspector will turn a blind eye."

"Thank you, Mum," said the lad, gratefully, and he looked very young, and very tired. I caught the eye of the inspector, who raised his eyebrows at me and jerked his head towards the hall.

I took the hint. "Let me just fetch your coat," I said, and he followed me from the room. We stood together by the hatstand at the door, where his raincoat and brown homburg hung.

"It's very concerning," he muttered, "very concerning. To be blunt – I have no way to be certain your brother is dead. There's no evidence. But why would Mrs Corbus lie? Do you believe her?"

"I… I'm not sure I do. Sometimes I think – no. I'm not sure." It was a difficult thing to admit, when my instinct was to give her my unwavering support.

"Is the marriage happy?"

"Perhaps that's the wrong question," I said. "Or, at least, it won't tell you what you need to know. It's more important to say that even if things were not well with his wife, Reynold would never willingly leave his laboratory for any length of time."

"A driven man, then."

"Absolutely."

"They're not the type for suicide," Price mused.

"What can we do, then?"

"Your brother will need to be missing for twenty-four hours at least before I can start a manhunt." He stroked his moustache, and "We'll return tomorrow and speak to the boy. Maybe he'll shed some light on it. And I'll bring a doctor friend of mine. A psychiatrist. Keep a close eye on Mrs Corbus. Frankly, I'm more concerned about her than him. Men, successful men, can sometimes take it into their heads to live the high life for a few days, and forget their responsibilities. I've seen it before. When we field telephone calls from distressed wives, we know where the blame lies."

"Indeed," I said. It seemed plausible. And yet it did not strike true.

Price shrugged on his raincoat, and put his homburg on with precision. "Davis!" he called, and the constable arrived at speed, revived by the tea and biscuits. "See you at nine tomorrow morning, Mr Corbus. Try to get some sleep, if you can, sir. I've a feeling it'll be a long day."

I watched them return to their Wolseley, which had seen better days, and gave a short wave as they drove away. Then I returned to Patricia. She had taken a seat on the chaise longue, her legs crossed at the ankle before her as she sipped her tea.

"Poor Constable Davis," she said. "He was dead on his feet."

"Do you think you could sleep?" I asked her.

"I'll try," she said. "And you, you should try too. I always keep the guest room ready, just in case you pop in."

"How kind." I did not want to leave her. I crossed to the tray, poured myself a cup of tea.

"Phillip."

"Yes, my dear?"

"Thank you for coming."

What a ridiculous sentiment: a phrase repeated up and down the country, every day, meaning very little, wheeled out without thought. But she meant it, I could tell. She had not been certain I would come when she called me, and I felt ashamed that she would have doubted it. I had left her alone for too long, once Bucky had left for school. Supporting her should have been reason enough to come, even though I had kept my distance for reasons I did not want to think about.

"However I can help," I said, slowly, "I will."

"You are a real friend." Her voice shook. I could not look at her.

"I am your brother," I said, and I thought she might break then, confide in me, let me comfort her. But she remained separate, sitting upright with barely a tremble in her hand as she raised her cup to her lips. The moment passed.

"I'm not mad," she said.

"Absolutely not."

"I might go on up, then."

"I'll see you in the morning."

I waited until she had left the room, taken the stairs. I gave it time. Eventually I risked going up.

Bucky's room was at the end of the upper hallway; I had to pass the master bedroom and guest rooms to reach it. I walked as quietly as I could, to stand outside my nephew's room. I didn't knock. I opened the door, just a crack, and looked in.

The curtains had not been drawn. The window was half-open, and moonlight filled the room, throwing all the furniture into sharp relief, as if drawn in pen and ink. The bed was made, the sheets pulled tight. Bucky's suitcase was on the floor, open, his clothes in a jumble within. A ruled notebook lay open on his small desk. He had drawn an orb web spider there, in clear observant detail. It reminded me of the drawing he had made years ago, but I could see a more mature force at work for this sketch. Eight long legs jutted from the bulbous abdomen, which held upon it the marks of that defence mechanism: a disconcerting pattern of a watchful face. Hairs, fine and long, had been stroked delicately upon the paper, with a steady hand. What an artist he was becoming.

Through the window I could see the stretch of lawn, the lake. The woods, rising dark and thick, beyond.

The sleep after a headache can be deep. If anything occurred in the night, I did not hear it.

When I came down for breakfast, not long after seven, the staff had already arrived, and breakfast was on the sideboard in the dining room. Order had returned: the usual comings and goings of the house, just as I remembered. For a moment I could believe Bucky would come down, bouncing with energy, a very young boy with no worries or concerns, and Patricia would follow him, smiling at me as we shared his enthusiasm for a day spent together ahead. Maybe even Reynold would make an appearance before heading for the laboratory, grabbing a slice of toast before starting his work. *What are you doing here?* he would say, in his usual brusque manner, then not bother to listen to the answer.

But no.

I selected a pikelet, some bacon, a boiled egg. When I took my place at the table, there was a letter, propped up next to the plate, waiting for me. My name was written on the envelope in her fine hand, and I opened it to find many pages, each one carefully filled in long sentences. It must have taken her the whole night to write.

Part Two

Dear Phillip,

I'm waiting for you to fall asleep. I have no idea how long that will take. Do you barely sleep at all, like your brother? Do you doze lightly, or are you lost to the world until another morning comes? How little I know about you, and you about me.

I'd much rather you didn't waste your energy on trying to understand me much, or to find me. In the hope of making you see the sense in that, I've decided to spend these last few hours in the house writing down precisely what happened to Reynold. I'll try to imagine what questions you'll harbour and answer them as best I can. Hopefully this will leave you able to get on with your own life. In this house if you like; it always did belong to you more than to me. Please, do feel free to take the house, use it as you will. But rip out the laboratory: that would be my suggestion. Redecorate. Put the portrait that hangs above the fireplace in the large lounge out of view. Destroy it, if that would make you feel better, although I think I know at least enough about you to think that's not an action you'll take. I only mean to make you understand that you owe us nothing.

Except, Phillip – try to take care of Bucky, a little.

I wonder: are you asleep yet?

I don't know where to start.

Reynold once said to me, when I asked him how his ideas came to him: *One idea leads to another. You begin at the beginning, and you take a step in any direction. There are no mistakes, because each step leads away from the start, towards the conclusion. You cannot know one from the other until you make a start. So you make it.*

When we started our married life, I had never felt better. I so enjoyed travelling to Paris straight after the ceremony. What an exciting city that is. I had worried about the timing, due to my regular pains, but luck was with me and it all fell perfectly. Oh, Phillip, I should explain – forgive me, the last thing I wish to do is embarrass you, but perhaps it sheds light on what happened later... and what is honesty without a touch of embarrassment? I suspect the two are inseparable, so here goes: every month I have terrible pains, a woman's complaint, and nothing can be done about it. I've seen doctors. None of their cures work (more fresh air, less fresh air, more exercise, less exercise) and their opinions often hint that I am peculiarly sensitive to aches in that area, rather weak in constitution if you like, and the best course of action would be to... well, they've never put it in these terms exactly, but I think it boils down to toughening up. They all agreed that it would be very unlikely that I could conceive, or be able to carry a child to term, given my disposition.

This is not a secret, and I was not unfair. I told Reynold all of it. In fact, it was one of the very first conversations we had.

He came to a shoot my father was hosting at the Kent estate – I rather think he felt bullied to attend, since my father had ordered the installation of a hundred ThinkBulbs in his factories up north – but it turned out Reynold was a terrible shot so he sought out the library and found me there, under the painting of the house, a Siberechts, that's a bit of an heirloom. He pretended to examine it with a critical eye, and I pretended not to notice. I was just at the end of my pains, and feeling rather useless. I'd picked up my embroidery and had a book about Greek myths open before me; I was copying a picture of a centaur, trying to pick out the form with needlepoint.

"Those are marvellous stories, aren't they?" he said.

We chatted for a while, but he had no gift for light conversation and things soon turned serious. Have you ever noticed that when you know someone very little, or not at all, you put your own thoughts and feelings upon them with an ease that is missing with friends, even family? Perhaps I imagined him entirely sympathetic that day. It's possible that his mind was elsewhere as he listened. But I think I'll choose to be certain of his attention then, and his love since. He really did love me, and he adored Bucky, in his way. I will always keep that comfort, to the end.

He was already well known as a great inventor. Even I had heard of him. I asked, "Can you solve any problem you put your mind to?"

He held my gaze with that earnest sincerity of his, and said, "Perhaps."

"That's wonderful. What a gift."

"It scares me," he said.

I was disarmed by his honesty, and wanted to offer him reassurance. "If somebody has to solve all the problems of the world, I am glad it's you."

"Really?" He smiled. "Then the only question that remains is what problem I should solve first, if any."

"What an amazing choice to be able to make."

"You think so? How would you choose one issue of our time over another, Miss Alrington?"

I put down my embroidery and picked up the book. I turned to another illustration I had attempted to copy, but it had proved too complex for me: Zeus, on his throne, looking down upon the world, with a lightning bolt in his hand. "If one is a god, one should act like a god, and please oneself entirely."

"That is the only logical conclusion one can come to, isn't it?"

I thought he was joking. I liked him enormously for it.

"Call me Patricia," I said. And I told him of my complaint. It was freeing beyond measure, to speak of it to a man who was almost a god. In return he spoke of you, and your own illness, and of how the human body is perhaps the greatest of all mysteries.

He never said it was a mystery he wanted to examine, and so I cannot be disappointed that he never did turn his attention to our ailments.

Remember, down by the car that afternoon, Phillip, when you said to me he couldn't possibly be a god because of the mean tricks he used to play upon you? I suspect the opposite: I hold it as proof.

At the end of the afternoon he left, and I was oddly bereft, thinking I would never see him again. Beyond that, I was aghast at myself, the more I replayed our meeting over and over in my mind that night: to have told so much to a stranger! Or would it be worse if he was not? If he became an occasional visitor to the house, and looked upon me every time with pity behind unfailingly polite expressions? I veered between scenarios, dreading them all, but this unhappily imaginative state did not last long, for he returned the following weekend, without an invitation, and told my father of his intention to spend time with me, if that suited. How very Reynold that was. I was flattered. Even then, I had some idea of how much of a valuable commodity his attention outside of the laboratory was.

A fast courtship gave way to a proposal. *You take a step in any direction.* Except all directions ended up being in Reynold's direction.

At least it was a direction away from Kent.

I have loved Reynold well — well enough to give me nightmares forever more, although I wonder… I wonder if I'll ever dream again. I hope not. He has made me wary of everything the mind can conjure, and what our imaginations can make of us.

He envied you, Phillip. Not the illness, of course not that, but the ability to make art. An act of creation beyond the scientific. When I told him of my pregnancy, I was anxious. He had married me knowing I could apparently not conceive, and he had seemed more than content with that. Had he preferred me that way, wanted a future without children? To keep his concentration unthreatened, perhaps? It was such a relief when he was all delight, exclaiming, "We must celebrate!" Then he fussed over what form the celebration might take, instantly protective, deciding against champagne or dancing. Eventually he said, "I know," and led me to the morning room, and we sat together quietly for the evening, before the fire. He did not even glance towards the door, nor mention his work once. We talked about maybe returning to Paris one day, as a new family, once the baby was born. "To the Louvre," he said, teasingly. I had loved our walk around its hallowed halls.

There is a famed sculpture in the Louvre – no doubt you know it – called The Winged Victory of Samothrace. It is said to represent a goddess, but when I first looked upon it, gazed up at it from the foot of a large staircase, I thought it an angel, a warrior, a woman of power. A strange thought, since it lacks its arms, and a head; how hard could it fight for itself, or for others? I reminded Reynold of it. I don't know why it came to mind at that moment.

He nodded, as if he understood. "There is a craftsmanship, a translation from mind to hand to medium, that makes humanity a noble animal," he said. "The person who carved that marvellous sculpture is connected, intimately, to all other creators through all time. I saw a figure that conquers time itself. That is the victory. And all artists share in it. Even my brother, with his small paintings and ambitions. And you – you thought yourself incapable of creation but look at you, at this moment. How beautiful you are."

"I'm terrible at art," I told him. "All I can manage is a bit of needlepoint."

"That's not quite what I mean," he said, smiling.

I realised he talked of the baby to come, and I said, "Darling, you're at least half as responsible for that, so you're an artist, too. But then, you've always been an artist. Look at your inventing."

"Inventing," he said, and he sounded weary, disdainful. How dismissive he was of his achievements. I wondered, then, if ThinkBulb had brought him any happiness, or if it was all people claimed it was: an unworthy thought for a wife. I reached for something to say to cheer him.

"Surely inventing and painting are just two parts of the same thing? It's only how you've chosen to express it. I think you must be one of the most creative men alive, Reynold. I'm certain of it. But you express it differently."

I saw it land within him, then: an idea. He soaked up my words. "Yes," he said, slowly. "Yes."

"Besides," I said, as a joke, "if you want to be an artist instead, all you have to do is pick up a brush and practice for twenty years."

"Now that would be a change in career!" He smiled.

I think it very likely that he started work on Ceredex the morning after that conversation. I did not know the details of it, naturally. He was wary of saying much about it, beyond that he had a new inspiration, and besides, I was kept busy with my pregnancy. My health declined. Eventually I was ordered to bed rest, and Reynold employed two nurses, lovely women who came in every day from the village, and they took excellent care of me throughout. I read, and sewed, and grew more bored with each passing minute.

Bucky did not arrive into the world easily, but when I had recovered a little I found it to be a very special time. My boy brought me such joy. How vital he was, thriving, and Reynold thought him a miracle. He even left the laboratory for a while, but once Bucky started to crawl he seemed to lose interest, and he returned to his experiments.

I leaned on you, then, Phillip, I must admit. I felt my heart lift when your car drove up to the house. Your pride in Bucky, your willingness to spend time with him, hours and hours of play and healthy attention: all of this sustained me, even as I struggled to return to a life of regular bouts of debilitation, for my complaint redoubled at that time. How difficult it is, to be free of pain for a short while, only to find one must shoulder the weight of it once more. Please don't mistake me – I will always appreciate the life I had. A life with no need to work, with all material comforts given to me. If only I could have appreciated what I had before it was gone. Does it make us terrible people, Phillip, if we long for a life without pain, and forget to be thankful for what we have?

Never mind. I know you would defend me, but you don't yet know the whole truth. Here it is: Reynold did not kill himself.

Phillip, Phillip. You must believe me that it will be better for everyone if the world thinks that he did. I can see no other way around it. The shame of such an act will be infinitely easier for you to bear than the horror of the truth.

It took Reynold eight years to complete Ceredex. During that time we came to live separate lives. I saw him for a brief spell in the evenings, when he emerged to wish Bucky a good night, but even that small contact stopped when Bucky left for school: a decision Reynold took himself, regardless of my feelings. But I am too emotional, and it became clear to me that it was best for Bucky to be away from that. I saw the good it did him, to be free of us and the dour atmosphere of this house. For myself, however, I was terribly lonely, and my complaint grew worse for that, leaving me miserable. I should have taken up a new hobby, charity work, anything. It's very difficult to make plans knowing that you might simply be forced to break them for the sake of your health. Instead, I kept to the house. I expected nothing from Reynold, and I thought he expected nothing from me. But all that changed a week ago.

Has it really only been seven days since he came into the front parlour at around three in the afternoon? I looked up from my book and found him standing in the doorway, still wearing his white coat, his hair standing stiff from his forehead with beads of sweat visible upon his face.

"I've done it," he said.

He was wild-eyed, agile. He flung his arms wide and strode in, then paced upon the rug. "I've done it. Come see, Pat. Come see." He reached for my book, threw it to one side. I took his hands and allowed him to pull me up; I had to hurry to keep up with his steps as he led me to the laboratory.

I'd taken meals down to him on trays before, once or twice, but this was different. I must admit it was a thrill to encroach into his private world at his invitation. The overhead lights were very bright, and he took me past the cluttered table, filled with his papers and devices, to the corner, where a new contraption stood, next to the row of filing cabinets. That was when I got my first look at Ceredex.

I found it an unprepossessing sight, I will say; I will admit this only to you, Phillip, but it looked a little like a hairdryer at a salon! I did smile, a little, at the ramshackle nature of the helmet and the stool, but he did not seem to notice.

"What does it do?" I asked.

"It's easier if I show you." He swung back one of the clear screens and stepped inside, then took a seat on the stool, glancing up to make certain his head was in alignment with the conical helmet suspended above.

"There's no danger," he said. I took a few steps back anyway. He reached up to the helmet – there must have been some sort of activation button or switch on its side – and there was a surge of electricity, or some sort of energy, deep and strong, that I could feel through the air. The hairs on my arms and the nape of my neck stood on end. The lights of the laboratory flickered, then steadied to an uncomfortable brightness, and the helmet began to glow. A blue effect, like a flame, licked from its rim to the crown, then up the wires to the beam above. I watched with my heart in my mouth, wondering if this was the intended effect, or if something had gone horribly wrong. Should I call out? But Reynold's face remained calm, his eyes closed, his expression serene, somehow. I was caught in that indecision when it came to me that something on the other side of the laboratory was scratching. The sound grew in volume. It was rhythmic, and there was a persistent quality to it.

Reynold remained perfectly still on his stool.

The sound became very loud, could not be ignored. I searched it out, took a few steps towards it. In the corner of the laboratory stood another screen, but this one was made of a green fabric, suspended from a metal frame with casters at the bottom. I knew the type, having seen them in hospitals now and again. Thick wires ran from Reynold's invention across the floor, underneath the castors, to whatever lay behind. The scratching undoubtedly emanated from it.

I crossed the room, pushed back the screen.

Behind it was a small plinth, rather Grecian in style, not unlike the ones we had seen in the Louvre. Upon it sat a lump of red clay, of a good size, half-shaped into something resembling a human head and shoulders, although none of the features were discernible. Perhaps it's in our nature to see something of that size and shape and assume its similarity to the human form. Two lengths of metal, joined together by some sort of rivet at a central point to create an elbow, jutted from a small gap at the base of the plinth. The extended limb moved over the clay relentlessly and, wherever it touched, small shavings as light and delicate as feathers fell from the face. For it was carving a face, I could see its emergence from the red surface. A crude likeness: eyes, nose, mouth – but all the features together did not create a recognisable person.

You would know more about this, Phillip, but there is something about the positions of the features that creates an artistically accurate portrait, something in the juxtaposition, the skill of the artist, that I had not properly appreciated before that moment, and the machine Reynold had created simply did not have that skill. The arm went on, cutting away at the clay with its ruthlessly sharp finger, and the overall effect of the sculpture did not improve. In fact, it began to elicit a feeling of disgust in me. By the time the arm came to a halt and retracted into the base, I felt quite repulsed by the result. A child could have done better.

The lights flickered, dimmed. I did not take my eyes from the sculpture. Reynold came to stand beside me. I was glad not to see his expression when he perused the result of Ceredex's labour.

"No," he breathed. "I thought I'd found a solution." He knelt, and began to gather the shavings of clay, pressing them together to form a ball.

"Darling, what an incredible machine," I said.

"Is it?" he said, dully. "Who is this a likeness of, Patricia? Can you tell me that?"

"I… um… Anthony Eden?"

"It was meant to be a self-portrait." He squashed the ball of spare clay into the face, digging his fingers into the crude features, obliterating them.

"Oh." I tried to think of supportive things to say, aware I had to tread carefully, speak lightly. We had never discussed his failures before – only his successes. I knew he much preferred it that way. "I'm certain it's nearly there, darling. Such an achievement."

"Useless." I'd never seen him defeated. It was a new kind of pain for me. "Ceredex is designed to take latent artistic talent and amplify it, utilise it to create. It's an extension of ThinkBulb, do you see? It should provide proof of artistic ability. But this – this is no better than a child would do. It's a joke, Pat. A parlour trick. I've sunk eight years into this. Eight years." He put his hands to his face. For a moment I thought he would cry. I reached out to him, and he brushed my touch away. "Maybe if I…"

he muttered, and he was lost to me once more. He returned to the booth and began to tinker. I think he had already forgotten I was there.

"Good luck, Reynold," I said.

I left the laboratory and returned to the morning room, retrieving my book from the floor.

He did not come to bed that night, and I was not surprised. I lay there, thinking about how I had felt in the moment of his defeat, when he had been close to turning to me for comfort. I had enjoyed that pain: a shared pain. It had brought me happiness. Did that make me a terrible wife, to want Reynold to be brought low? I should have told him, at that moment, to return to work, rather than praise him insipidly. But how could I urge him to give more, when it meant I would receive less? Honestly, I felt rather cheated, for I felt he had made it purely for himself: to unlock or improve some aspect of himself that he saw as lacking, although I did not. His creativity was never in doubt, was it? Although he did not possess the ability to see beyond his own intended use of Ceredex – but it came to me then, had he not already invented a device that could bring much good to the world, even if it was no Michelangelo? Even with my limited imagination I could envisage that many people would gain benefits from it – people that Reynold had not even considered. People without limbs, without a way to express, to touch, to feel. Ceredex took thought and turned it into action. It was astonishing.

Reynold had never considered that, just as he had never considered even trying to aid my own complaint.

I thought back to the conversation we had shared on the day I met him, in my father's library.

If one is a god, one should act like a god, and please oneself entirely.

I think that was the moment I realised he was utterly selfish.

His selfishness was still very much on my mind the next day, and I did not expect to set eyes on him for days, perhaps weeks, but when I walked into the dining room the following morning there he was, looking out of one of the long windows with a view over the lake, drinking tea.

He turned to me when he heard me come in, still frowning from whatever thought he had been lost in, and said, "Pat, I need your help."

My first instinct was to refuse him nothing; after all, that's what a marriage is: a promise to be there when one is called for. I don't think I even properly understood that, at the time. It has become much clearer to me since.

"I've found a way around the problem," he said. "A method to make Ceredex work."

"It does work," I said. I remember it was a grey morning, misty. I could only just see past the lake, to the line of the woods beyond. "It has so many uses already -"

"Not to people who don't have artistic brains," he said. "There's something – some part of the mind – that can't be unlocked without physical practice."

"Isn't that how it should be?" I came to stand beside him; I wanted him desperately to understand. "If you started now, Reynold, and sculpted every day with your own two hands for many years, could you not learn how to make something marvellous, and feel a huge sense of achievement because of it?"

He stared at me. "What do you think Ceredex is?"

I couldn't explain it to him. "I realise this isn't the same thing at all, not when you want to make a masterpiece, but I have embroidered every day since childhood, and I've become so much more able than when I started out. Or – look at your brother, at his talent –"

I knew instantly I'd said the wrong thing.

"I'm not a child, Patricia. You think I haven't thought of this? We're talking about the same thing, if you'd only listen. Your embroidery – this is what I mean. You have some artistic talent, obviously, even if it's only stitching. That area of my own brain is not powerful enough to use Ceredex to its full potential, but yours might be."

"What do you mean?"

"I have another Ceredex – a prototype. I've connected it to the finished version. With you sitting in one booth and me in another, Ceredex will take your artistic skills and my imaginative thoughts, and sculpt something spectacular. I'm certain of it." His eyes were very bright. "Do you understand? You can give me what I'm lacking. We'll be the perfect pair."

"You want me to sit under that helmet?"

"While I sit under another one. You've seen how it works. It's painless. It'll be done in a moment." He put his teacup down on the table and held out his hand.

"Right now?"

"No time like the present," he said.

I wanted to take his hand. I wanted to be the wife I had promised to be. I cannot say for sure that it was not that new seed of disdain, planted within me, that made me hesitate. "I wouldn't be any good at it," I said.

He dropped his hand. "You don't wish to help me?" I don't think it had ever occurred to him that I would hesitate.

"Darling, ask Phillip. He's the true artist."

Reynold shook his head, with a vehemence that was almost childlike. "I'm not interested in Phillip's aid. I'm interested in yours. But you don't wish to give it."

I did not reply. I could have said: *I'm angry at you.* Or: *Why can you think of nobody but yourself?* I don't know why such words did not come to me. I went to the sideboard and selected half a grapefruit, and a cup of tea, with a slice of lemon. I badly wanted him to speak. Still, he said nothing as I sat at the far end of the table and started on my grapefruit. It was very fresh, very sour.

He left the room. I did not watch him go.

The following day he drove to the school and brought Bucky home.

I hadn't realised he had gone from the house until his return, when Bucky came running across the lawn to find me. I was in the rose garden, and there he was – how happy he looked, and tall, too! Solid. All that rugby, I suppose. "Mother!" he called,

"Mother!" and there was a crest of happiness, the likes of which I had not felt in years. He cannoned into me, and nearly knocked me over, and I wrapped my arms around him and closed my eyes, almost convinced it was a dream.

When I opened them again, Reynold was strolling over the lawn towards us, his hands in his pockets, looking quite pleased with himself. All my happiness vanished.

Bucky confirmed my fears. "I didn't want to come at first, there's a house match tomorrow, but Father says I'm essential to his experiment, so I had to come, didn't I? I'm essential now." He struggled with the long word, managed it with pride.

"Reynold," I said, as he came within earshot. I kept hold of Bucky tightly. "Reynold, take him back to school. Now."

I don't know who was more surprised: him or Bucky.

"Now, you're building this into something it simply is not, Patricia," he said. "You've seen Ceredex. You know what it does. How could that harm anyone, in the least?"

"Take him back. If you need help with your experiments, I'll provide it. I'll give you my – artistic brainwaves, or whatever it is you want. You shall have it all. But not Bucky."

"But Mother," protested Bucky, "I want to help. I want to be part of the experiment, I don't mind, I promise." He pulled away from me. His face, so dear to me, was a picture of disappointment, but I could not explain. I think he saw, then, that I would not change my mind. He ran down the lawn, towards the lake. I knew he was heading for the woods.

"Bucky!" I called. He did not stop.

"Let him go," said Reynold. "It's a real disappointment to him. He talked of nothing else in the car."

"Because you put the idea into his head. How could you? Without even –"

"It came to me that perhaps I didn't need a mind cluttered with existing notions of artistry and craft through needlepoint or painting, or so on, but a mind before such preconceptions form. A purer connection to creative thoughts, if you will. Everyone's mind must be open to the possibility of artistic imagination at first, surely?"

"He knows nothing about it, Reynold. He's a boy. He likes rugby and cricket and hide-and-seek, and drawing, yes, he draws things he finds sometimes, but not – oh – can't you see that it would be wrong to use it? To take something from him that he doesn't even know he has to give?"

Reynold was indignant. "I take nothing from anyone! I never have."

I looked up at the house, an imposing outline in its perfect setting, and thought of the rooms within, the wealth of his family stretching back through the generations, all his possessions, and his life – a life he had promised to share with me. I knew I could not make him understand, and I despaired.

But then he squinted up at the sky and said, "You think I have a closed mind, that I think only I know best. But that is not how one becomes a great scientist. You think I'd go against your wishes, and shut you out. You, his mother, my wife. It's as if you don't know me at all, and that's my fault, I'm aware of it. Another of my shortcomings. Oh, Pat, you hardly trust me, and that is painful to me. Let's try to mend that."

Possibly I didn't quite believe it, this sudden change of heart, but I wanted to, oh, how I wanted to. And I knew it was my duty to try.

"I'd like to," I said.

We agreed to put all matters of the laboratory aside for a day or two, and spend this unexpected gift of togetherness with Bucky, as a family. At the end of that time, Reynold promised to return Bucky to school, and only asked humbly that I would think once more about the experiment, in a calmer frame of mind.

Honestly, Phillip, it was the best of times, and Reynold was as good as his word. We played croquet and I watched the two of them at tennis. Bucky was improving quickly; he gave Reynold a run for his money.

Then came this morning. We went to the nearby park and enjoyed ice creams, and even took a trip in a rowboat around the pond, which nearly ended in disaster when Reynold dropped an oar and the manager had to row over to retrieve it for us. But my husband laughing, laughing loud, relishing the discovery of some feat for which he had no talent – it made everything better. I had hopes, then, he might understand that he did not need to be a genius, an inventor of international repute, a figure at the forefront of science above all else. He could be a husband and father – and a brother, naturally! – and that would be enough for us all.

How cold the house is tonight.

Surely you sleep by now.

I must write it down, I must, or there will never be peace for you, and you deserve that, my dear, dear

Phillip. How I longed for a brother as I grew up: a protector, a confidante, bound to me by name, by blood. You have become that to me, and more, and I thank you.

I do not think you'll be shocked to learn that Reynold could not keep his promise to me.

The park, the rowboat. After that we returned home, all in good spirits. Only a matter of hours ago. How strange. It was the servants' night off. Bucky wanted a last run round the woods in the fading light, so Reynold lit the fire in the larger lounge, and we held hands, sitting side by side on the carpet with a bottle of wine and some leftover ham and tongue pie to share, eating wedges of it with our hands. It was quite the picnic. We laughed about how Bucky had offered to jump in and fetch the oar for us, even though he was worried about what might be in the water.

"What a brave little man he is!" I said. "And he's only just learned to swim."

"How could he have thought there were monsters lurking in parks in Oxfordshire?" Reynold said. "One wonders what they're teaching him."

"He'll be pleased to get back to all that nonsense tomorrow, but I will always cherish the memory of today. Thank you, darling." I kissed him deeply, and he returned it with fervour.

"You go on up," he said. "I'll fetch Bucky in, and put him to bed. Then I'll be along."

"All right."

And that was the last time I saw Reynold alive.

Nothing but glad thoughts crossed my mind as I took my bath, soaking for longer than usual in scented water, enjoying myself enormously. Then I prepared for bed and lay in the dark, thinking one thing over and over: *we can be a proper family. We can be happy together.*

I must have fallen asleep for a time, just a light doze: I didn't want to be snoring when Reynold came up, but it had been such a strenuous day. Still, I don't think that more than an hour had passed before I snapped fully awake, aware that something, somewhere, had made a sound.

I lay there. The room was very quiet, the windows cracked open, with the net swaying, just a little, with the breeze. I was absolutely, incredibly alert. What had that sound been? A voice, or the grind of metal? Something high and long. Not human.

The tick of the clock on the bedside table was loud. I tried to listen past it. The hall light was still on, its light a line under the door.

I had to find out what had made that sound. Feeling utterly afraid, but knowing no good could come of hiding, I threw on my nightgown and slippers, walked into the hall, and took the stairs down to the ground floor where everything was still. A terrible thing: I did not even check for them there. I knew where they would be.

Down to the basement. The door was closed, as usual. I had expected no less. I opened it slowly, without knocking, wondering how loud a noise would have to be to reach me from this room, the walls filled with the thick wires of the ThinkBulb, and the large beams overhead that should have deadened all sound.

I don't know if you have ever entered a room in which everything looks, at first, to be in its usual order, but you then become slowly aware that something is profoundly wrong. Perhaps you felt it when you walked into the laboratory yourself this evening, Phillip, but I think I've done a good job of cleaning up. Here's the thing – I didn't see it. Not immediately. The mess on the walls, in the corners. All over the table. I was only aware that something was different. There was the prototype, the second Ceredex machine, now wired up next to the original; well, I knew Reynold had planned to do that. At first glance I thought the crude clay sculpture was the same too, but how could it be? I had seen him gouge its features, reshape it to blankness. This had to be another attempt; I could not see it clearly from across the room. But I was alone. No Bucky, no Reynold. Only myself and my imagination.

My eyes returned to the sculpture. The curve of the back of the head caught my attention. It was carefully shaped. But not exactly human.

I took a few steps forward. All the lights were on. I spotted a cobweb across one of the wall lamps behind it. Seeing one: that was the turning point. The realisation. More cobwebs, some fine, white and stringy, in clumps. Hanging from the ceiling. Others, in the corners, in the classic pattern, radiating out, creating a lattice to trap prey. The sculpture was untouched. The top of the table, too, but underneath – how could I have not seen it before? Between the legs was a barrier of webs, as thick as spun lace. There had to be an infestation. The thought made me shudder. I stopped walking forward, edged away from the table. The face of the sculpture upon its plinth came into sight. I saw the quality of the work. It was highly skilled. The face was instantly recognisable as Reynold's own, except there were bulbous protrusions, fresh markings. The eyes: how they stared. All the eyes.

If this was what lurked in Reynold's mind then he had been right: I really did not know him at all.

I heard the quick, light skittering of some creature crossing the floor behind me. The sensation of being watched was awful in its intensity. I did not dare to move. I looked at the filing cabinets, the coatstand, the wires. One of the helmets, within the new device, had been wrenched from the beam, and was only half-attached to the ceiling. And in the first device, I could see the stool had been upturned. Low down on the transparent screen was another web, radiating from a white central point. No – it was a crack. Someone, or something, must have hit it with great force, smashing against it.

I kept watching.

The table, that mess of white material under it. I thought I discerned a shape within, at least as tall as me. A cocoon? The thought came to me that Bucky would know what it was, and it took me far too long to put the webs with the shape. Unforgiveable, to have been so stupid. I ran to it, dropped to my knees, pulled at the substance. It was sticky, but not ferociously so. I had to stop and rub my hands on my nightgown to clear the stuff away. I worked on it for what felt like an age, aiming at where I thought his head might be, from the shape. All the time I felt that presence somewhere behind me, watching me, but I could not give in to the screaming voice in my head demanding I run, run away, *far* away.

When I managed to bare the face, push back the strands to reveal the features... It would be easy to write that they were unrecognisable, but that's not true – I knew him instantly. My husband. But how shrivelled he was; lipless, the eyes open but shrunken deep into the sockets, dark, in contrast to the grey-white of his hollowed cheeks, and his teeth were bared, very white and slabbed, like the teeth you see in the mouth of an ancient skull. It was useless to think anything could be done. He was so very dead. Everything vital had been sucked from him.

The skittering came again, closer this time, and I ducked, out of some instinct, I suppose. Something flew past me, inches from my arm. I got to my feet and yelled. I don't know why, or what I shouted, but I kept going, I could not stop.

Bucky came out tentatively from behind the white coat on the stand, moving his limbs with great care. For a moment we simply looked at each other –

or, I think he looked at me. His back was to me at first, then he turned. He was undoubtedly my son, yet also the living embodiment of the sculpture upon the plinth, alive and breathing and no longer quite human. The glass jar you gave him – in which to keep his specimens from the wood – still hung around his bruised and twisted neck. He should not have been alive. I can't explain it more than that, Phillip, it's beyond me, or perhaps I lack the will to try.

After a time he moved to the door, and left me alone.

Whatever I write further will make you hate your nephew and godson, and I could not abide that. I want you to be certain that this was a terrible occurrence that Reynold brought upon himself. I begged him not to use Bucky in his experiments. All the blame lies with him. Perhaps I was truthful, after all, to say he killed himself. Something terrible, some flaw, lurked within him and came out when that sculpture was made. You saw it for yourself. That flaw has altered my son.

There's not much more to write.

I made a decision, on the spot, to clean up the mess. I despaired of moving Reynold's body, but it was surprisingly light, and easy for me to drag up the stairs and out to the lake, or perhaps I was filled with some kind of mad strength. No, I have never been strong, we both know that. I think blood must weigh a lot, and with it all gone from his body he was nothing more than a shell. He took a long time to sink into the water. I changed my clothes, threw out my night things. Then I telephoned you. I did all this to take care of Bucky as well as I can, and I ask you, please, Phillip, with all the good in you, do the same. You and I both know where he will have gone. Protect him.

If you are not asleep by now you never will be.

I am going. I must leave all this to you. I am not strong enough to stay.

Yours, forever,
    Patricia

PART THREE

My first thought was to find her.

She might have gone back to her father. No, no – she did not want to be found, she would go to no place familiar to me. She was right; we barely knew each other, after all. Brother and sister by marriage, friends by circumstance, and I couldn't imagine the first place to look.

Bucky, however: I certainly knew where to look for him.

It was impossible to believe her strange story but she had written it with utter candour. It was true to her. A horror had lodged in her mind. My immediate hope was that whatever happened to Reynold had created some sort of temporary breakdown, a delusion within her. Could it be nothing was as she described? To her, Reynold had become a monster: a megalomaniac who was prepared to experiment on his own family. But the brilliance of him, if he had managed to create a machine that turned brainwaves into action – was that not incredible? How could he have failed to see the wondrousness of that, even if it could not create an artistic masterpiece? Whatever did such a word – masterpiece – even mean, if it was torn free from the years of study that should accompany it?

And yet it did not seem strange to me that Reynold would think artistry could be objective, and he would be jealous of those who seemed to possess skill in that area, simply because he did not have it himself. And if Patricia's suspicions were accurate, and ThinkBulb was not all it was said to be, then that would be another level of shame Reynold carried. Not an artist at all, but a charlatan,

I remembered the Christmas I had been given a sketchbook and pencils, and had drawn our dogs, Hunter and Seeker, asleep by the kitchen hearth. I had been praised for the effort by our mother, even though it had not been exceptional: how could it have been? Such skills take practice. I had found him later that afternoon with my new gift, attempting to replicate my work. When he saw me watching, he had thrown the book across the room. But boys are prone to such destructive outbursts. We built towers from our bricks and knocked them over with glee; if one of us built a den in the woods the other would take a stick to it. I had thought such games long behind us. Now, I was not so sure.

Reynold, dead.

Not a god. Only as flawed as the rest of us. To survive that terrible war, to find his end in the room he loved best in the world, at the hands of his own son. If Bucky continued to have hands at all. It had to be a mistake, some awful mistake. There was only one way to be certain if Patricia had lost her mind.

I checked my watch. Three quarters of an hour remained before Inspector Price, Constable Davis, and the psychiatrist arrived to get to the bottom of this. I sprang from the table, breakfast untouched, and used the French window to reach the terrace, affording me a view over the lawn. It was a fine morning, with a clear vista down to the lake, and the woods beyond. The quality of the light was spectacularly clear: a perfect painting day. I tried to picture Patricia dragging a cocoon of white strands, Reynold's drained body within, across the grass, all by herself. How light would a body be, if drained of blood? I shook my head, tried to focus, took the steps to the lawn. The grass was soaked with dew. It sparkled in the sunlight, seeped into the cuffs of my trousers.

She had claimed to clean a mess of webs from the laboratory, and, if that were true, she had done a good job of it. No obvious proof of her story remained. The sculpture, though: that awful countenance, carved with undoubted skill. It was beyond Reynold's ability, surely. Perhaps she had carved it herself? She had artistic leanings. A nightmare vision of my brother's head and shoulders: could he have been that much of a monster to her?

I reached the lakeside. At the edge of the calm green water, by the bullrushes, I found a flattened patch of reeds, and a slip of mud, churned up. But that could mean anything. I examined the water but could not see into its depths. There was only my own reflection, showing a quizzical frown. How like Reynold I looked at that moment, wearing the very same expression he would adopt when puzzling at a scientific mystery.

I took another glance at my watch. Half an hour remained.

I ran around the edge of the lake to reach the woods, where the first of the yews grew, casting their twisted shadows over the ground. I paused on the threshold, aware I was about to step into shadow. My own strained breath was very loud in my ears. There were no other sounds to steal my attention. No wind, no rustle of leaves. No birdsong. How strange. No birds sang within the woods.

Only a few strides in, I saw the first of the webs. It was an impressive construction, stretched across the dirt track between two tree trunks. What a specimen, with its radial spokes and long lines. I would have pointed it out to Bucky on one of our walks and we would have marvelled at it together, and searched for its creator. I moved around it, leaving the track only to blunder directly into another web. The strands clung to my face, my hair. I swatted at them with my hands; their tacky residue stuck to my suit jacket. I rubbed my hands on my trouser legs and pressed on, returning to the path, unnerved by the silence. But I saw no more webs until I reached a clearing where the sunlight could reach down and touch the leaf litter and damp growths of the ground. A sublime spot for a den; I had made many there over the years, with Reynold as a boy, and then with Bucky. There was a fallen log at one end that could be lifted to reveal interesting insects beneath. Above, the trunks formed a kind of curved wall through their spacing that felt formal in construction, although they had only grown that way through chance, or natural design. They were tall ash trees, thinning at their crowns, where the light could play through the leaves to create a dappled effect.

Between these trunks were too many webs to count, and each one had been spun crazily, free from the usual patterning, to make designs that at first seemed nonsensical, as if their creator was working to no rhyme or reason, but the longer I looked at the light filtering through the threads, the more I could see purpose behind them, and it brought to mind a strong memory that could not be denied: standing at the font with tiny Bucky in my arms, a newborn waiting to be baptised, and Bucky's gaze caught by the rays of the sun, his eyes filled with light, colour: the wonder of the moment.

It was undeniable. The webs were in the shape of the stained-glass windows from the small church in the village. I could discern figures, picked out in thicker strands, almost opaque in places, and the lightest touch in others. In some places the designs were marred by larger balls of thread, suspended like baubles. I realised they were birds, trussed up in silk.

I saw one with its head dangling while its body was held in place, one eye dull, its neck feathers ruffled in permanent disarray. But there were many more, too many to count.

I stood perfectly still. Where the light touched, it illuminated such breath-taking skill to recreate a place holy and special to me. It was utterly beautiful. And I was caught within it, as surely as if I had stepped into the sticky hearts of the designs. I realised I had been corralled, directed to stand at this very spot by the placement of webs. I was precisely where the weaver of this work of art wanted me to be.

Everything in me sprang to high alert. I dropped to a crouch, an instinct perfected by the war, and began to edge away, back along the path. I did not dare to look at what lay behind me. Instead, I fixed my gaze on the webs: and there he was. I saw him, perched high in the crook of a branch, in one of his own creations. His back was to me. But he was looking at me, too, through new eyes, nestling in his hair: a row of unblinking eyes, bulbous, fronded with long dark lashes, level with his ears. His neck was discoloured, purplish and swollen, and wiry golden hairs grew there too, quivering in the light. He wore the tattered remnants of short trousers and a striped shirt, which had stretched around his lumpen torso, and his limbs had bent in strange angles, snapped backwards, to enable him to cling to the branch with an ease very far from human.

"Bucky," I said. "Bucky."

From around his neck hung the glass jar to which I had affixed a rope, years ago, when we had first started visiting this wood together: the jar in which he had kept his living treasures. I could not see what was trapped inside it, but I felt certain that it was watching me too, poised, ready to smash itself against the glass.

He shifted, took a tentative step down with one arm, which flexed and straightened with careful precision.

I felt a surge of pity. There was no fear in me. I wondered: *is he in pain?* I would have spared him that. His head swivelled. He presented his real face to me, the dear face I loved. My Bucky, his eyes wide and clear, as if an awe. Dark spots had formed on his cheeks in symmetry, creating the markings of a camouflaged predator. I knew that pattern. And I recognised that same expression he had worn as a baby, caught in the wonder of the light. He looked at me directly. I felt he knew me.

He opened his mouth and I thought he would speak. Call for help. I could not bear it, closed my eyes, and heard something stir the branches on my right. I had to look. A stream of silk had traversed the clearing with ease; I have no doubt he could have hit me with it if he had wanted to. But instead he had aimed for a colourful swatch of material that fluttered there, pinning it in place. I recognised the green leaves, the yellow tulip print: Patricia's scarf. The one she wore on the day of our first lunch, when we sat together on the terrace.

I continued to back from the clearing, moving softly, slowly. Bucky watched me with his boy eyes. I had to hope I did not blunder into one of his webs; I had the feeling that could have triggered his new instincts. When I had put some distance between us I risked turning my back on him, but kept my even pace, trying to retrace my steps exactly. The silence was intense, but my head was clear, free from any ache, and I felt young, ready to act. I blamed him for nothing. I did not want to have to hurt him if he sprang for me. Imagine, thinking that I could hurt him. I reached the place where the trees met the lawn and saw the lake, the house beyond. It was only the sight of that normalcy that undid me. I ran. I ran as fast as I have ever run, the fear suddenly within me, I was stung with it like a venom, and I did not dare to stop until I stood on the terrace, panting.

Only then could I afford to think.

I could guess some of the story: Reynold had fetched Bucky from the woods, interrupting his hunting for specimens to draw. He had taken the boy down to the laboratory with a fine example of an orb-web spider still hanging from his neck. Perhaps Reynold had not noticed; he would have been hasty, determined to conduct the experiment without Patricia's knowledge. I could picture the two of them sitting in the booths, eager to see the results.

Then something had gone wrong with Ceredex. Or perhaps it would be more accurate to say something had gone right: it had taken the information offered to it, the brainwaves of father, son, and that unwanted third party, the spider, to create a sculpture. But the process had an unexpected consequence; it also mingled their minds in some terrible way, combining their very essences, and Bucky had been changed.

Better to think that than to believe that Reynold had harboured some inkling of what might happen to his son, and that had been his purpose all the time. Transformation. Or that Bucky, filled with a cold hatred, had taken revenge for the mutation exacted upon him. And the thought of what creature might lie in the jar, still hanging from Bucky's distorted neck... No, that I would not think about. Never. Never.

Take care of Bucky: Patricia had entreated. Her scarf lay in the woods.

I preferred to imagine that she had gone far away, that even now she was travelling to a new life. The headscarf, well, it must have slipped from her head as she hastened away, and blown on the breeze to her son, who might find comfort in seeing it, and stick it to a branch so he might keep it with him.

And so I would do as she asked, and protect him.

I slowed my breathing, checked my watch. A quarter past nine. The police would have arrived. I tried to calm myself, practised a smile. I rehearsed a story in my head. Then I entered the house, and found them in the hall, waiting for me.

We stood in the laboratory, the four of us, gathered around the sculpture. A faint smell lingered in the air, metallic, almost sweet. The overhead lights were blazing. I had not bothered to turn off the electricity this time. Patricia's doubt of the ThinkBulb had seeped into me. Besides, what difference could it possibly make, now? If it triggered a headache I would accept I as my lot. I could change nothing. I was very calm.

Inspector Price reached out as if to touch it, then dropped his hand. "What do you think, Doctor Marshall?"

The psychiatrist was an older man, balding, bespectacled, with a serious turn to his mouth – rather what one expects for a doctor, even one of the mind, but with a red spotted handkerchief poking from his top pocket that spoke of some cheeky unconventionality. He had greeted me with enthusiasm in the hall, declaring himself a fan of my latest exhibition.

"An imaginative mind is not necessarily a disturbed mind," Marshall said. He walked around the sculpture once more. Constable Davis stepped back and cast an eye over the contents of the table: the stack of paper, and the instruments of Reynold's trade, test tubes and a microscope. Was there anything out of place? Perhaps only the tidiness. Patricia had written of cleaning the place to spotlessness. Again, I could see no trace of webs, nothing of the grisly events of last night.

"What does this invention do?" asked Davis.

"He does not talk about his work to me," I said. "He never even mentioned that he took up sculpting." I resisted the urge to explain in any detail. It would be best to appear as unaware as possible.

Davis crossed to the first booth, his attention on the helmet that had been half-wrenched from the ceiling. "This seems to have come undone," he said.

"I can't say how it's meant to look, I'm afraid." What else had Patricia written? A crack, on the clear screen – I looked at the second booth and saw it immediately. It was just as she had described. A radial pattern, emanating out from the force of the blow, leaving fine white lines. I crossed to it as nonchalantly as I could and stood with my back to it, shielding it from Price's view.

"And you say you woke this morning to find Mrs Corbus had also gone missing? With their son? She left no word of where they might have gone?"

"Nothing at all. Do you think Reynold may have been in touch last night? Telephoned, perhaps? I'm a deep sleeper. She might have woken Bucky and taken him to a reconciliation." I allowed myself to sound hopeful. It was easy to do. How I wished it could be true.

"Without informing anyone she was leaving?" Inspector Price sniffed. "That sounds unlikely, if you don't mind me saying so. She struck me as quite a conscientious woman."

"Love makes fools of us all," I remarked. "I think it possible, actually. She's the romantic type."

"And you called me here for a consultation," added Doctor Marshall. "That's not your habit unless you suspect some form of mental issue."

"I thought the lady might be upset, but not…" He shrugged. I don't think he had the words to explain the feeling that something was deeply, profoundly wrong. I had it too, but had to pretend otherwise. For Bucky's sake.

"You know, this really is remarkable," said Marshall, his attention still on the sculpture. "A force, a vigour. There's an urgency to it." He looked up, spoke to me directly. "Art soothes a tortured soul, does it not? I don't believe this could have relieved the maker."

"So you do think there's evidence of a disturbed personality here?" pressed the Inspector.

"I would need to communicate with the person for some time to make such a diagnosis. Hours of back and forth are needed, careful observation, awareness of interaction. There's an art to it. I can't simply stare at a creation and see the soul of the creator within. And with no opportunity to speak to either husband or wife in this case, I can do nothing to help."

"So you see no cause for alarm in it, then, Doctor?" said Constable Davis. He returned to the sculpture. "I think it's a terrible thing. I didn't sleep well last night for looking at it."

"It makes you think uncomfortable thoughts?" Marshall asked the young man, who stood to attention, his expression suddenly guarded.

"I didn't say that."

Marshall laughed. "I may have an explanation for that, at least. Isn't this room fitted with ThinkBulb?"

"It is indeed," I said.

"I thought so. I thought so. I've had the most illuminating thoughts myself since entering. Encouraging brainwaves may have the side-effect of expanding the mind into more….challenging ideas, shall we say? Maybe your thoughts spring from that, Constable. You know, I'd love to investigate how ThinkBulb could be used with patients with certain psychiatric conditions. Has anyone investigated that yet?"

"I don't believe so. You might well be the man for the task. Shall we return upstairs and discuss it?" I pointed to the door.

"Certainly, certainly," said Marshall. He continued to mutter on about the prospect as he led the way from the laboratory, with Davis and Price following. I waited until all three were at the door before moving from the crack in the surface of the booth – the one piece of evidence of a violent encounter that could not be cleaned away.

Price waited for me, and gave me a shrewd, quizzical look when I reached him. "You seem much better this morning, sir."

"For now," I said. "The headaches come and go."

"Shock can do strange things to people. I…" He leaned towards me. The others were already on the stairs. "I suffered dreams myself, after the war. Bad ones, you understand. Marshall may seem a bit unusual but he helped me. I thought perhaps he might do the same for Mrs Corbus, or even yourself."

I switched off the laboratory lights. We stood in the darkness together. That moment was the closest I came to telling all, fetching the letter, asking Price to help me make sense of the events that had taken place. He was a good man, I felt certain of it. It even seemed possible that he might believe Patricia's story, and come to the woods with me, and see Bucky's plight for himself.

And do what?

If he thought Bucky more boy than spider, then the child was a murderer by law – and this was a man who believed in the law.

If he thought Bucky some sort of twisted, grotesque arachnid then he would demand it caged. Possibly even exterminated.

The moment passed, and I did not speak.

"There's not much I can do if you don't wish us to investigate," murmured Price. "It's a waiting game, the way I see it, with all three gone and no cause remaining to sound an alarm. I'll have a quick word with the staff before I go, sir, just to be sure, but the best guess I can make is that they're together somewhere. On holiday, perhaps. Let me know when they get in touch. Do you think it a likely outcome to be sooner rather than later, knowing your brother?"

"Why not? But honestly, Inspector," I said, "I hardly know him at all."

I followed them up the stairs. No headache came. They stayed for an hour longer, and we said our farewells just before lunch.

I had a friend send a postcard from a Jamaican villa in Reynold's name, and arranged a few other things to make it look as if their idyllic reunion had taken place. It gave me pleasure to do so – to see it in my mind's eye, as a possibility. An alternative path that was not taken, if you will. When they did not return after a month I raised an alarm, but by then I was ready. No suspicion fell upon the house. I saw Price again, and Davis, and the events of that night when we first met were treated as the act of a jilted wife, led to unsound thoughts. The police in Jamaica searched, found nothing. Naturally. They had never been there.

I returned to the family home, and I'm ashamed to admit I could not quite carry out Patricia's wishes. I did not destroy Reynold's inventions. Not even the sculpture. I started studying the basics of science soon afterwards. I wish to understand what he did; perhaps that is the next best thing to ascertaining why he did it, or if it was all some terrible mistake. Every day I learn a little more, and I hope that in twenty, maybe thirty years, if I am lucky, I will have answers. And so all his works are sitting beneath me, at this moment, as I write this at the desk in the morning room. They are my foundation. Sometimes I stand in his laboratory, left untouched, and think of the thick wires in the walls and the sharp blades in the base of the plinth that sculpted his likeness.

Five years have passed. The headaches come frequently, often with intense emotions that I cannot control. Sometimes I feel rage, the kind that used to sweep over me when I fought for my country; but what am I fighting for, now? There were times when I took up a shovel from the stables and headed out to the woods with the thought of ending the life of the creature, stuck between the states of boy and spider, surviving on a diet of birds and small creatures. It never once attempted to hurt me as I approached with care, watching for its sticky traps, and as long as it kept its glassy orbs upon me I felt I could strike, revenge myself against it. But then it would swivel that golden body, freed from rags to reveal thick hairs upon its broken limbs and swollen abdomen, to show me Bucky's eyes instead, amidst the markings, and I saw Patricia in them, and heard her voice begging for my help, and knew I could not act against the creature.

Now, when my rages come, I forgo the shovel and take up my painting equipment instead. I walk down to the lake and set up where I can see its silken creations through my binoculars. I try to replicate their beauty and their horror on canvas, as best as I can. The webs remain stunning, evocative to me, but not since that first day do I see a resemblance to something of the human world within them. I think about the stained glass windows, the light of the little church falling on to Bucky's new eyes, often, and I wonder: did he *remember* that? Is he still that newborn child, inside?

Last month I presented my latest exhibition of paintings inspired by the creature's webs. Eminent critics called me an imaginative genius. I can see why Reynold liked such epithets. It's good for one's self-belief, even when one knows it is untrue. One could say that Bucky is the real artist of the family, spinning his designs from his corruption, creating visions that incorporate the bodies of the dead.

And who made Bucky what he is today? Why, Reynold and Patricia, of course. I realised, while standing in the laboratory next to Price, caught in the indecision of confession, that this is the very truth of the artistic soul. Creations are made. They, in turn, begin to create. There is no way to control what will come into the world. And here I part company from Dr Marshall's theories, espoused on that terrible day. I absolutely believe that, yes, we can see the evidence of the suffering, tormented mind in such creations. We can see it because we all experience it. Even if we can never know another human being well enough to understand them, even if we think ourselves above them or beneath them but never equal to them, we can be certain of this: we all suffer.

It's rare that I manage to make the journey to London to check if another painting has been sold. It always amazes me that people buy them. With every sale I ask to check the name and address of the buyer. I like to think that it might lead me to a small, safe cottage somewhere, and if I knocked on the door Patricia would answer, admit me, tell me that she escaped that day and left only her bright scarf behind. That she has been happy every day of her life since, and my arrival makes her happier still. This story begins and ends with her.

ABOUT THE AUTHOR

Aliya Whiteley's strange novels and novellas explore genre, and have been shortlisted for multiple awards including the Arthur C. Clarke award, BFS and BSFA awards, and a Shirley Jackson award. Her short fiction has appeared in many places including *Beneath Ceaseless Skies, F&SF, Strange Horizons, McSweeney's Internet Tendency, Lonely Planet* and *The Guardian.* She also writes a regular non-fiction column for *Interzone* magazine. She lives in West Sussex, UK.

ALSO FROM NEWCON PRESS

ANIMALS – Geoff Ryman

A powerful new novel from the multiple award-winning author of *HIM, Was* and *The Child Garden* The chilling tale of a family caught at the heart of a terrifying and transformative epidemic; an astonishing fusion of beautiful writing and pure horror as the world we know falls apart.

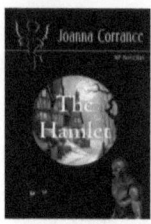

The Hamlet – Joanna Corrance

A fabulous tale that dances between horror and science fiction with an added dash of weird, *The Hamlet* is a mosaic featuring the inter-linked lives of inhabitants of a very peculiar rural community during the time when 'things got strange', and shows us the consequences of that strangeness.

Rowany de Vere and a Fair Degree of Frost – Chaz Brenchley   Rowany has taken up service on Mars. As a spy. Her mission is to escort a defector across the hostile surface of Mars, pursued by Russian agents. Success will require every ounce of her skills, but she is Rowany de Vere. Of the Colonial Office.

Into the Dark – Patrice Sarath

This debut collection from an award-winning filmmaker and author living in Texas gathers her finest short fiction, adding a brand new story for good measure (which is currently being adapted into a film). Contemporary fantasies, deep space skulduggery and so much more…